I0586320

A collection of steampunk short stories

COGS AND CONSPIRACIES

A collection of steampunk short stories

KAREN J CARLISLE

Kraken Publishing

Cogs and Conspiracies
A collection of steampunk short stories

Cogs and Conspiracies © 2023 Karen J Carlisle

The moral right of this author has been asserted.

All rights reserved in all media. No part of this book may be reproduced, stored or trans-mitted in any form, or by any means, without written permission (except under the statu-tory exceptions of the Australian Copyright Act 1968).

This is a work of fiction. All characters and events in this publication, other than those clearly in public domain, are fictitious. Any resemblance to real persons, living or dead is purely coincidental.

Cover design and internal design Copyright © 2023 Karen J Carlisle
ISBN: 978-0-6458151-0-8

NATIONAL
LIBRARY
OF AUSTRALIA
A catalogue record for this book is available from the National Library of Australia

Also available separately as eBook (edition 2).

This book is written in British English.
Printed in Australia.

Typeset in Times Roman 12pt.

Published by Kraken Publishing.
www.krakenpublishing.com
www. karenjcarlisle.com

For the steampunk community,
who welcomed a broken writer and
helped me rediscover the joy of whimsy.
I hope these stories give you all a little joy as well.

Short Stories

ive short tales set in a world of steampunk and alternate history, with adventures from England to the Antipodes. Here be villains, gadgets, mechanical creatures, secrets and conspiracies. All in time for tea.

Stories from the world of
The Adventures of Viola Stewart and
The Department of Curiosities.

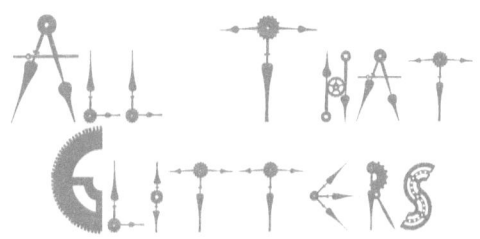

1840s-50s, Adelaide Hills

The ground shuddered. A roar thundered from the depths of the mine. Metal scraped. Gears ground.

Puffs of grey smoke rolled out of the tunnel's entrance. Streaks of black stained the clouds. The greasy smell of oil filled Alice's nostrils.

The ground shuddered again. A blast of sulphur stung Alice's eyes. Tears rolled down her cheek.

She sniffed at the air. Black powder?

Alice scanned the buildings along the edge of the camp – the tool shack, generator shed.

Empty.

The heavy spanner slipped from her hand and clattered onto the transport rail at her feet. She slammed the lid onto the Gas Extractor.

"Soo Lin?"

The earth moaned.

Dry air caught in the back of Alice's throat. Her lungs convulsed, expelling debris.

"Get out. Now!" She straddled the narrow rail line, grabbed the switch handle and peered into the swelling mass of smoke.

Another rumble bellowed out of the tunnel.

Where are you?

The handle writhed in Alice's hand. She braced her body and fought to calm the gyrations. Her elbow tendons twinged.

The rail vibrated through her boots.

Alice scrutinised the smoke. Shadows hissed and clacked amongst the plumes. The vibrations intensified. Shadows coalesced. A string of white smoke pierced the gloom. A petite woman, in tan overalls, stood on a box-like railcar, wrestling with the vehicle's lever. She wrenched it backwards, almost throwing herself to the floor.

"It's about time," said Alice.

Soo Lin frowned. "You duck."

"I'm a what?"

The railcar shuddered to a stop. Soo Lin jumped off the railcar and somersaulted behind the generator shed. Long dark braids whipped against her back as she landed silently.

Alice snatched up her spanner and turned to face the tunnel.

"What have you done?"

"Not me," replied Soo Lin. "A dragon."

"A what?"

"I throw *huo yao*. Dragon gone." Her brilliant white grin peeked out from an enormous pair of blackened goggles.

Alice scanned the railcar. It was empty.

"Not the whole box?" she asked.

"If ignore dragon he will eat you," she replied.

"Always a proverb," said Alice.

Soo Lin shrugged.

"There's no dragons in Humbug Scrub, Soo Lin. Snakes, kangaroos, Howlers yes – but nothing as big as a dragon. They just don't exist."

"It have big shiny eyes. It growl. It breathe smoke. What you call it?"

A roar thundered out of the tunnel.

"Down!" yelled Soo Lin. She grabbed Alice's trousers and yanked her behind the shed.

A low rumble shook the guts of the mine.

Alice slipped the goggles over her eyes and peered around the edge of the shed toward the tunnel. The sound grew louder, creeping closer to the surface, and cracked through the entrance with a deafening boom.

Alice dodged back behind the wall of the shed, hoping it would hold under the concussive force.

Clods of earth rained on her head. The smell of sulphur caught at the back of her throat. She glanced at Soo Lin and covered her ears.

"What have you done?" asked Alice.

Soo Lin's eyes widened. Her gaze dropped to the ground.

Alice adjusted her goggles and squinted in the direction of the mine.

Choking clouds of brimstone belched from the tunnel and rolled along the floor in a cumulous wave. Filter masks jiggled on the shed wall, as if to vex her. Alice spluttered and snatched one from its hook.

"Bloody hell." The curse crackled in Alice's throat. Her

eyes watered. "My mine!" She wiped the moisture from her nose and eyed Soo Lin.

Soo Lin remained crouched behind the shed, her eyes still fixed on the ground. She shook the dirt from one of her braids, coiled it behind one ear and pinned it in place. Her fingers untangled the other braid, shook it and coiled it behind the other ear, as she stood slowly.

"Are you all right?" asked Alice.

Soo Lin swallowed and nodded.

"Come on, fire up the Gas Extractor. We need to check the damage." Alice shook out the mask and surveyed the area.

Soo Lin remained behind the shed.

"Soo Lin?"

There was no answer.

Alice turned to face her friend. Soo Lin stood, staring at her feet, her shoulders slumped.

"Soo Lin, please look at me."

Soo Lin dragged her gaze up and locked her attention on Alice's chin. The lines around Soo Lin's eyes deepened, creating crevices that crept along her forehead. Tears welled up along her eyelids. Her mouth crinkled. Alice had not seen Soo Lin this upset since she first met her, after her husband had absconded to the gold fields.

A wave of dread flooded over Alice's body.

"Are you injured?" Her heart sank into her stomach. "Is there something you're not telling me?"

Soo Lin shook her head and sniffed. Her gaze fell back to her feet.

"Sorry. I panic. It is my fault. I will pay –" Soo Lin's voice was muffled. She reached into her pocket.

Not injured. Alice's muscles relaxed. Her heart slowed. Thank God.

They shared a common bond. Alice's wretched husband had abandoned her, lured by easier pickings in New South Wales. Soo Lin helped her run his neglected mine. They made a formidable team; with Alice's engineering skills and Soo Lin's knowledge of explosives, they had delved beyond the shallow copper deposit.

There's a wealth of gold down here – if we could only catch our thief. Alice straightened her shoulders and took a deep breath. Her friend was worth more than broken beams or a collapsed mine. Alice turned to Soo Lin. She spoke slowly.

"Don't worry. Accidents happen." She placed her hand on Soo Lin's shoulder. "Come on; let's go find your dragon."

Alice rubbed her ear, still feeling the effect of the explosion. She pulled her mask over her face and strode into the smoke-filled tunnel. The swirling cloud obscured her vision. Her boot scraped the metal rail. She reached out her arm to steady herself, groping the air until her fingers scraped against compacted earth.

A loud clank of metal gears echoed down the tunnel behind her. Soo Lin cursed in Cantonese. The Gas Extractor responded with a long hiss and chugged into life.

A gentle breeze dragged smoke past Alice's cheek toward the tunnel entrance. She ran her fingers along the wall as she inched further into the tunnel.

Footsteps padded up behind her. An eerie smudge of yellow light bobbed along the tunnel. Her muscles tensed.

A gas lamp? Fire! What if it set off another explosion?

Dark patches of clean air formed in the tunnel.

"Is the gas lamp safe?" Alice asked.

Soo Lin nodded.

"No *huo yao*." She sniffed the air. "Gas gone. Safe now."

Small wisps of smoke curled around Alice's ankles, as she sucked filtered air through her mask. Soo Lin's father had taught his daughter everything he knew about fireworks and explosives. She wouldn't risk their safety.

Alice's muscles relaxed.

Alice and Soo Lin trudged down the tunnel, following the vein of copper as it curved down to the gold deposits. Alice rounded a corner, and almost slammed into the pile of boulders. Debris blocked the tunnel, spilling over the twisted rail.

"Bloody hell!"

"Perhaps we find way through?" Soo Lin smiled weakly, picked out a few smaller rocks and tossed them to the ground.

Alice nodded. She scrabbled up the debris to reach the smaller rocks. She pushed, pulled and wriggled them. They wouldn't budge. She leaned toward the edge of the rubble and tested the rocks there. Warm air trickled over her hand.

Alice chuckled. She wriggled her fingers.

"There's air coming through a crack here. Perhaps the explosion breached the mine?" she said.

"Another way into tunnel?" replied Soo Lin.

Alice nodded. "We need to go rabbiting."

"Rabbiting?" asked Soo Lin.

"We're looking for a very large rabbit hole," replied Alice.

Shadows crept across their camp. Alice glanced upward. Grey clouds crept in from the south.

A faint clop ground on the loose stones.

"Looks like rain," said a voice.

Hot breath rushed over Alice's neck. A horse whinnied near her ear. She recoiled from the sound. She turned to see a stout, well-dressed man atop a thoroughbred horse. He tipped his hat in Alice's direction.

"Good afternoon, Mrs Drake." He wheeled the horse, turning his back on Soo Lin.

"Is it, Mr Roach? It's not that grand from where I stand. I'm delighted to hear you are having a more fortunate one."

Soo Lin lifted her finger to her lips and shook her head. Alice dusted off her trousers and cleared her throat.

"And to what do I owe the pleasure of your company?" asked Alice.

"I saw the smoke. I thought I would check my neighbour was safe," He tapped his hat back in place.

"How thoughtful of you," said Alice.

"My offer for the mine still stands." He glanced back to the smoking tunnel, put his gloved hand to his mouth and coughed. "Unless there is extensive damage, of course."

"It's nothing serious," said Alice.

"I worry for you, Mrs Drake." The reins fell from his hands as he gestured toward the surrounding trees. "All alone in the bush."

"I'm not alone."

"No one to protect you from the natives." He leaned forward in his saddle. "When will you come to your senses? A mine this size cannot be run by a woman. You need men to work it."

7

"I have Soo Lin."

Roach eyed Alice and wrinkled his nose.

"No wonder your mine has been unproductive."

"Only because someone is stealing our gold."

"Theft? That's a serious accusation, Mrs Drake." Roach raised an eyebrow. "I hope you have proof to back up your story."

Proof?

Alice's eyes narrowed. She straightened her shoulders and glanced at Soo Lin.

Soo Lin shook her head. She raised her hands, curled her fingers and made hopping movements, like a rabbit. Alice bit the corner of her lip, trying not to smile.

"Why bother yourself with such an ill-fated venture when you could afford to take a house in town, relax and concentrate on more…" He eyed her dusty clothing and raised an eyebrow. "... Lady-like pursuits. I'm going to Steventon: If there's anything you need…"

Alice grabbed the reins and handed them to Roach.

"Thank you for the offer," she replied, as she slapped the horse's neck. Its muscles twitched. "We need no assistance."

"As you wish, Mrs Drake." Roach drove his heel into the horse's flanks.

Alice watched the horse trot out of sight. Soo Lin removed her goggles and squinted in their wake, her eyes two pale circles ringed with soot and dust.

"With money, you are dragon," said Soo Lin.

"With too much money, you're a worm," added Alice.

Soo Lin laughed. "You do listen."

Alice nodded and scanned the sky. "Looks like it will rain," she said

Soo Lin plucked up the lamp. "After rabbiting, we find proof."

Twigs snapped under Alice's feet. Branches snagged her blouse and scratched her arms, as she trekked through the dense scrub. She glanced behind her. Soo Lin danced her way through the undergrowth, avoiding entanglements.

Wooden talons scraped Alice's trousers. The branches snapped. The smell of eucalyptus filled the air. Alice breathed in the fresh aroma; the sweet, pungent smell filled her nostrils. She glanced up at the sky. The light was fading. Dark clouds hovered close to the hilltop.

"We should have fetched the oilskins," said Alice.

A chilled breeze washed over her face. A blob of rain fell onto her arm. Another plopped onto her eyelash and rolled into her eye.

Alice's foot rolled on the rocky ground. She rubbed her eye and blinked her vision clear. A wide crack snaked along the ground toward a shadowed clearing further down the gully.

"Our rabbit hole?" asked Soo Lin.

Alice scrambled to her feet and searched the scrub. She picked her way over the uneven ground along the crack. Soo Lin padded close behind.

"I would expect a lot more debris with an explosion," said Alice.

Alice stepped over a thick fallen branch. The ground collapsed under her weight. She sank into the damp, dark earth.

Cold sludge oozed into Alice's mouth and between her

fingers. Dirt trickled down her collar. Splashes encircled her in the dark. Her ankle throbbed.

Alice opened her eyes. The lamp lay on the ground a few feet away, its glass cracked.

Soo Lin picked up the lamp and examined the casing. She shook the lamp, twiddled the knob and lit the wick. A glimmer of light emanated from the mantle, sputtered then slowly filled the cavern with its comforting glow.

Pale yellow mud clung to Soo Lin's skin and weighed down her overalls. She rushed toward Alice. Thud, squelch. Frowning, she shook her foot; one slipper drenched.

Alice pushed herself up to her knees and spat out the offending mud. The air was cold and damp. There was a smell, like…

She blew flecks of dirt from her nose.

Like coal.

She surveyed the cavern. Dust danced in the faint shafts of light streaming from the jagged maw in the earth above their heads. Drips of rain thudded on the exposed roots and plopped to the ground next to Alice. Water seeped from a crack in the nearby wall and bled into puddles. Small wavelets rippled and glistened in the lamp light. The cylindrical burrow curved away into the darkness away from the mine.

"That's one big rabbit hole." Alice ran her hand along the walls. A deep furrow spiralled along its length. Was this the work of Soo Lin's dragon? Not possible. The surface was too regular. "I think your dragon went that way," she said.

Alice and Soo Lin followed the burrow further away from the mine into the darkness, towards the dragon's den.

The light from the lamp swung back and forth across the

burrow.

Left, right. Alice followed its movement with her head.

Left. Right. It helped her to forget her aching feet.

Left. Right.

Her chin itched. She rubbed her face. Dry mud crumbled over her hand. How much farther?

The light jiggled. Alice shook her head. Her ankle twinged.

"Light ahead," whispered Soo Lin.

"Turn off the lantern."

Alice drifted into the shadows near the wall and crept toward the opening ahead. Soo Lin followed in the dark. The burrow opened onto a cleared area of bush. Alice slipped behind a mound of earth to survey the clearing.

Leaves rustled in the tall gums. Shadows flickered across the ground, skittered up and over tin-roofed buildings and along the netted fence near the gums.

Moonlight danced over scattered dirt-encrusted mechanicals. A sharp-angled leviathan shrouded in canvas stood near a long shed, not far from the burrow. A wooden platform rose from the middle of the clearing. A long metal shaft ran down the centre of the contraption, pierced a maze of cogs and gears, and sank into a deep shadow in the ground below. Nothing moved.

On the far side of the encampment, a track wound down the gully back toward the road. Half way up the hill a pale homestead glowed in the moonlight. The windows were dark.

"It's Roach's mine," she whispered to Soo Lin. "Everyone's most likely down in Steventon whooping it up in the pub for the night."

Canvas slapped and tinked in the breeze. Alice eyed the covered giant.

"I wonder what's hidden under there?" She crept behind a nearby tree and motioned for Soo Lin to follow.

A faint crack echoed through the camp. Alice slammed her body against the trunk. Soo Lin rolled and landed next to her.

Who's there?

A melodic warble drifted down from the tree. They glanced up into the canopy. A small shadow flitted higher into the branches. It tilted its head back and sang again. Another warble replied from across the camp. Alice took a deep breath.

Bloody magpies. She chuckled and continued toward the canvas mound, peeking through a shed window as she inched past. Shadows of generator equipment were barely visible in the darkness.

Empty. Alice smiled. They were alone. She continued toward the canvased curiosity.

Several tarpaulins had been lashed together to cover the monstrosity. Alice grabbed a corner and peeked under the covering. A faint whiff of coal dust wafted upward. A domed portal stared blankly back at her.

"Soo Lin, bring the lamp." Alice peeled the canvas away from the bulk to reveal another domed portal on the opposite side, this one cracked.

Soo Lin held the lamp closer. A pointed, screw-like nose jutted from one end. The glass domes glistened and winked at them.

Shining eyes.

Soo Lin gasped.

"I think we've found your dragon," said Alice. "It's a mechanical digger." She pushed the canvas further up the hull.

Scorch marks blackened part of the casing on the far side. Soo Lin ran her fingers along the marks.

"Your work, I believe," said Alice.

Soo Lin nodded and smiled.

"I knew it was Roach," said Alice. "He's been using it to dig under the mine and steal the gold from under us. The cad!"

"Our proof," said Soo Lin.

Alice shook her head. "No, he could move it before the Constabulary arrive. We need more." She eyed the homestead on the hill. "And I know where to get it."

She pulled the tarpaulin back over the digger and headed up the track toward the homestead.

The house was dark. More importantly, it was empty.

Alice tiptoed down the hall, checking the rooms as she went until she found Roach's office. A carved oak desk dominated the room. Sturdy bookshelves flanked the window behind it. A small curio cabinet stood beside a leather couch on the other side.

Soo Lin scrutinized the bookshelves.

Alice marched to the desk and sank into the soft, padded leather of Roache's chair. Her eyes widened.

"I could get used to this," she whispered.

Alice scanned the desk: a carved ink set and blotter, a diary, a ledger and a large quartz crystal currently being used as a paperweight. She rummaged through the drawers.

The bottom drawer wouldn't open. She leaned in closer. A small keyhole was hidden amongst the carvings. Alice eyed Soo Lin.

"You don't happen to have any more black powder, do you?" she asked, smiling.

Soo Lin placed the lamp on the desk and shook her head. Alice's smile slipped. Soo Lin grinned. She poked her finger into her bun, pulled out a pair of curved hair pins and presented them to Alice.

"Will these do?" asked Soo Lin.

She crouched in front of the drawer, plunged the hair pins into the keyhole and jiggled them. There was a satisfying click. She slipped the pins back into her bun and eased open the drawer.

"You're a wonder, Soo Lin." Alice scooped out the contents and laid them on the desk near the lamp. There were documents and papers, stuffed envelopes and…

She unfolded a large map, plopped the nugget on one corner and pressed the paper flat. A survey map. She traced her finger along the lines of the river, across the gully to…

"This is a survey map of our mine," hissed Alice. She folded the map and slapped it together.

Soo Lin frowned and handed her a letter.

Alice shoved the survey map inside her blouse and scanned the letter. It was an application for a mining license reallocation—

"For our mine." Alice crumpled the letter in her hand and shoved it in her pocket. "How dare he!"

"We have proof?" asked Soo Lin. "We go now?"

Soo Lin glanced out of the window. She grabbed Alice's arm and dropped to the floor, pulling Alice down with her.

"What—?"

Soo Lin thrust her hand over Alice's mouth and shook her head.

A beam of light shone through the window and ran across the wall. Alice held her breath.

Footsteps trudged toward the house. The light darted across the ceiling and ducked back out the window. The front step creaked.

Alice's arm snaked up the desk. She felt her way across the blotter, past the ledger. Her fingers curled around the quartz paperweight.

"Grab the lamp, Soo Lin. Get ready to run."

The next step squeaked. Alice jumped to her feet and hurled the quartz through the open window. It clattered across the stable's tin roof. The crunching steps retreated, sped across the yard toward the stable.

"Run!"

They dashed down the hall, jumped the steps and barrelled down the track into Roach's camp. Alice's ankle burned. She bit her lip and ran on, past the platform, past the digger, toward the generator shed.

Soo Lin dashed into the shed. The generator chugged. There was a clank. Soo Lin burst out of the door and launched herself towards the mouth of the burrow.

"A diversion?" asked Alice, as she ran past Soo Lin.

Soo Lin nodded and ran after her.

The shed whined. A shudder reverberated through the walls.

Boots thundered across the stones behind them. Shots cracked behind them, echoing around the gully. The shed door slammed.

Alice ran down the burrow. Ran into the darkness. Back to their mine. Soo Lin's footsteps padded past her.

A soft voice laughed.

"In shallow holes, moles make fools of dragons."

THE END

1860s-70s, Adelaide Hills

Wet linen brushed Eliza's cheek as she bent down to pick up a wooden peg. She hated washing, but the precious water did bring some relief from the dry heat. She lifted her face towards the hot, inland breeze and let the moisture evaporate. Cool water dribbled down her neck, and under her collar. She closed her eyes as it trickled down her spine. She dug her naked feet into the grass under the makeshift washing line, letting the damp blades tickle her toes.

The ground vibrated beneath her.

Eliza shoved the wooden peg into her pocket and wiped her damp hands on her skirt and snatched up the washing basket. Red dust had already begun to settle on the wet washing. The Diggers were back.

She strode into the cabin, scooped up her eyeglass from the kitchen table, and leaned through the window to examine the paddock.

Clouds of dust billowed in the hills, trailing a growing scar of earth undulating down the hill face. Her heart plunged into her stomach. Sarah hadn't returned from the food store where their water reserves were hidden. If the digging machine's tunnel breached the perimeter, and she was caught in the cave…

Eliza snapped the brass cylinder shut, and pushed away the thought. She mustn't get distracted; if she let the raiders breached the store, there was little chance they'd survive the summer.

She retrieved one of the metallic cylinders from the trunk by the back door, and marched outside to track the course of the raider's tunnelling machine. Its path turned sharply, just beyond the far paddock, and petered out where it had dived deeper to avoid the perimeter fence.

She grinned and hefted the Activator in her hand. It wouldn't help them this time. Still, she couldn't relax; the new perimeter hadn't been tested. If the digger had slipped past already, Sarah would be in danger.

Eliza flipped open a series of metal caps in the ground, as she circled the fence line, then returned to the veranda. She picked up a stone from the pile by the back door, threw it at the tin shed next to the cabin, and scanned the yard.

A quadrupedal mechanical made of brass emerged from the tin shed. It pawed the ground with its front limbs. Patches of tarnish pocked its surface where the lacquer had long since worn away. It tilted its cranium, mimicking a flesh-hound eager to obey its master.

She thrust out her arm and pointed in the direction of the barricaded entrance of a cave on the far side of the cabin. It turned and loped across the yard towards the cave.

Eliza felt the ground with her feet, searching for any hint of vibration to betray the digger's incoming direction. She had to activate the correct section of the perimeter as there wasn't enough energy to activate the entire grid.

The smell of dust caught in the back of her throat.

The heel of her left foot hummed. She spun around to face the east paddock. The fruit trees stood motionless. She lowered herself, keeping an eye on the paddock, and flattened her palm against the ground. Granules of dirt fluttered and tickled her skin. The digger was close.

She refocused the spyglass. Still no sign of anyth—

A puff of dust spurted into the air. Sparks crackled in the dry grass. A sharp, acrid stench of ozone followed.

Eliza's skin prickled.

The ground swelled. The white sheets jiggled on the rope line, threatening to dislodge the long, forked branch on which it was precariously balanced.

Blood throbbed in her ears. Her pulse raced. She glanced over her shoulder, and swallowed another mouthful of dust.

Sarah! Her silent scream reverberated through her skull. Her throat tightened. She couldn't hesitate any longer, or they'd both perish. She sucked in a deep breath and rammed the Activator into the hollow cylinder lying snug in the earth.

The ground buzzed. A wave of energy pulsed through the perimeter grid.

A gigantic metal spike burst from the ground. Jagged cutting wheels spiralled around its nose, spitting out clods of earth as it tumbled back onto the ground, less than a hundred metres beyond the fence. A cloud of dust unfurled skyward, hovered, then plummeted onto the ground and exploded outward, engulfing Eliza. A stench of barbequed meat followed.

She gagged, and jumped back from the fence. Grit

scratched her eyes, but she refused to blink, as she prayed for any sign of her partner.

A shadow formed in the haze. Hands batted away the gloom, forming eddies in the dust. Sarah spluttered, stumbled closer, and twisted her fingers in the air, spelling: I'm OK.

Tears slipped from Eliza's eyes, and stung as they trailed down her cheek. Her fingers shook as she replied: Perimeter worked.

The mechanical hound lurched across the yard to meet her. Its heavy tail thumped against her leg.

Sarah tapped her on the shoulder when she joined them. She grinned as her fingers moved swiftly and gracefully: It's still your turn to do the laundry.

THE END

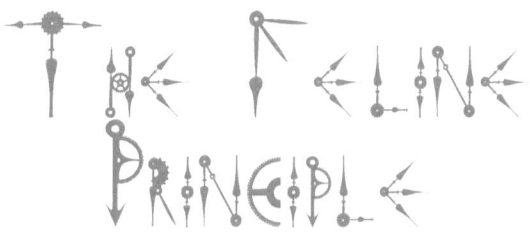

THE FELINE PRINCIPLE

1870s, London

Darkness embraced the alley. A cacophony of odours rose from the abandoned debris at the edge of the street. They lingered in the thick air, and seeped into the rising Thames fog, drowning in the smell of rotting fish and stagnant brine. Faint noises of merry-making drifted from an alley, broke against buildings and dissolved into the silent mist.

Metal clattered along the cobblestones, its origin hidden in the low-lying mist. A dark-clad man emerged from the fog, his feet breaking the established fog eddies.

Jacob Rowley was a merchant seaman, tall, muscled, practical. He pulled his heavy woollen coat tighter to ward off the growing chill of the river breeze.

Again, metal clanged on stone. Jacob halted, and turned his ear toward the sound. A blurred shadow materialised in the mist. A fluid obsidian form emerged - first one foot, then another - as if created from the fog itself.

Jacob lowered one shoulder, allowing his black duffel bag to slip onto the cobblestones. The feline padded forward until it reached the discarded bag, keeping a watchful eye on him. It circled the bag twice, and rubbed its cheeks against the leather.

"Fish?" Jacob chuckled. "You can smell it?"

The feline wound its body around Jacob's legs and purred loudly. A rhythmic pulse resonated through his thick woollen trousers. He reached down, cupped the feline body with his large hands and scooped it up.

"Hello, Lucky," whispered Jacob.

The intensity of feline satisfaction drowned out the drifting noises.

Jacob smiled. In his profession, cats were good luck and, if good luck had sought him out, who was he to ignore it?

He cradled the feline's face in his hands and stared into its amber eyes and. It Its stare commanded his undivided attention. A deep purring vibrated through his hand and permeated his thoughts. His muscles relaxed. Everything he'd planned for the evening slipped from his memory.

The world seemed irrelevant. There was nothing but calmness. And warmth.

The attic was always chilly at this time of the morning.

Sunrise was two hours away and the documentation seemed unending. Work was tedious under lamplight but there was little choice; by the time the building's gas pipes reached the attic, pressure had dropped significantly, resulting in a half-light with only intermittent spurts of useful light. Independent oil lamps lay salted on the trestle-table workbenches. Candles stood in strategic positions, for emergency use.

Scientific paraphernalia was strewn across one table - assorted stoppered vials in wooden holsters, tubes and beakers clamped in metal contraptions. Neglected experiments gathered dust. Various textbooks lay scattered across the other workbench. Pages danced in a breeze from the window, left open to allow gas and odour to escape.

Jars, containing metal and ceramic parts, crowded the ends of a second trestle. Brass springs lay to the left of a cleared area in the middle; work tools were fastidiously arranged to the right. A leather apron and gloves draped over the back of a chair.

Mr Christopher Cranshaw sat at a writing desk below the window. He adjusted the knob on his oil lamp; the gas was not behaving, as usual. Cranshaw was a small man, with brown hair, neat moustache, and gold rimmed spectacles. A bronze mechanical device curved around his left ear.

He checked his fob watch; reloaded his nib with ink and resumed his notes:

"Experiment #5 complete success.

Adult male subject succumbed to Feline Resonating Harmonic Inducer (FRHI).

Time: twenty-five secs post tactile contact; auditory manipulation of awareness. Skin contact required for full effect.

Confirms previous experiments.

Subject easy to approach. No precautions necessary, subject unaware and appeared in a trance state.

Resonator Disruptor (RD) successfully negated effects.

Note: subject B.01 survived third trial. No side effects.

Conclusion: Results confirm FRHI is ready for final stage. Subject: confirmed arrival residence 4.30 pm. B.01 to be deployed at 4.00 pm."

Mr Cranshaw replaced his pen in its holder and turned on the Resonator Disruptor. He donned his leather apron and pulled on his leather gloves, ensuring no flesh was exposed, and walked over to his bed wedged in the lower end of the attic.

Several felines occupied the feathered pillows; a tabby, a Persian, a white and two blacks. The Persian cracked open one eye, stretched, pawed a pillow and settled back into slumber. Mr Cranshaw smiled, unaffected by the modulated purrs.

He patted one of the blacks, picked it up and placed it in a basket, then removed his apron, placed the gloves and a revolver into his pocket, and retrieved his top hat. The final phase of his enterprise had begun.

⚙

Major-General Edward Sabine was an older gentleman who did not hold to the current fashion of mutton chops. Too fussy. He was distinguished and despite his years in the army, or perhaps because of it, he was well preserved. For the past year, he had served as President of the Royal Society, a position earned by his work as geologist, astronomer, and explorer, among other things.

He emerged from Burlington House, the current headquarters for the Society, donned his top hat and straightened his cravat. He hailed a cab and he made his way home, hoping for a quiet night.

Several research books, rested on Elizabeth Sabine's lap, engulfed in yards of red silk. She patted the geophysics textbook she had translated, and smiled. There were few colleagues afforded the honour of borrowing from the Royal Society's Records.

The books jiggled as the hansom cab tapped the curb. Elizabeth wedged the books under one arm, extracted herself from the cab and pulled her cream mantle over her shoulders as she hurried up the front stairs.

On the doorstep sat a majestic, jet-black cat; its coat glistened in the sunlight. Rich amber eyes met Elizabeth's gaze. It purred.

"What a beautiful creature!" A textbook slipped from her grip. Cats were the current fashionable accessory; how could she resist such a beautiful creature? She welcomed the feline, and coaxed it into the parlour.

Elizabeth sat on the chaise. Her visitor paraded around the parlour, surveying the room as if Master. Having marked each chair leg with ownership, the cat strode to its audience and caressed her skirts with its cheek. Seemingly satisfied with its undertaking, it leapt up onto her lap and circled twice before settling, maintaining eye contact during the entire manoeuvre.

A soft purr rumbled somewhere in its chest. Elizabeth squealed with delight. Her shoulders relaxed as she slipped her fingers into its silky coat. She caressed the fur, lost in a daydream, unable to concentrate, and a vague feeling there was something important she should remember.

The front door rattled as the Major-General knocked. The hour was late, the air was cold and he was impatient.

I'll see your pay docked, Molly. He remembered it was Molly's day off. Bother!

He searched his pockets. Nothing; he'd forgotten his key. He knocked again.

In the parlour, his wife dreamed of soft, sweet cakes and chocolate. A persistent noise echoed beyond the serenade of her new companion. She ignored it. The cat stirred. Its ear turned, as if distracted by the commotion.

The knocking grew louder, more persistent, and finally invaded her consciousness long enough to shake her from her reverie.

"The door!" Elizabeth rose to her feet.

The cat mewed, slipped from her silk skirts and landed on the chaise. Elizabeth shuffled to the front door.

"Elizabeth, I seem to have lost my key," said the Major-General.

Elizabeth shook her head.

"Impossible. I saw you take it with you, Edward," She unlocked the door and led him into the parlour, then relaxed back onto the chaise, scooped up the cat and set it on her lap.

The cat smiled. Elizabeth smiled. Edward did not.

"We have a little visitor," she sighed.

The cat purred.

Edward was a practical man, of Irish extraction. If his wife had insisted on procuring a cat, it would have to be useful.

He huffed. "It had better be a good mouser."

Elizabeth ignored him and sank her fingers into soft, dark fur.

"You know black cats are supposed to be lucky," she said.

"They're bad luck," he replied.

Elizabeth turned her head in to face her husband, rolled her eyes, and stroked the cat.

"How could something so beautiful and warm be unlucky? Come, sit by me and pat it. It will calm your nerves."

The purring grew louder as Elizabeth scratched the cat behind its ear.

"It sounds like one of those damned mechanicals, trying to start and not cranking over." He settled into his favourite chair by the fire.

"Oh, how droll you are, Edward. It's divine."

Edward frowned at her, opened the newspaper with a flap, and positioned it to block the scene.

The cat continued to purr. Elizabeth closed her eyes and let the sound wash over her.

⚙

Mr Cranshaw witnessed the Major-General's return, and searched for a vantage point. He tip-toed through the garden and craned his neck around a window, to spy his quarry.

The velvet curtain was slightly ajar, allowing him a partial view of the gas-lit parlour. The Major-General's wife sat on a velvet chaise, still attired in a red silk afternoon gown.

Mr Cranshaw smiled; no woman of her rank would willingly neglect to change for supper. On her lap sat Feline Subject B.01. Cranshaw grinned. Definite tactile contact. The Feline Resonating Harmonic Inducer appeared to be functioning as designed.

Direct observation of the Major-General was difficult; however. Mr Cranshaw surmised the Major-General had succumbed to the invention; one touch and continued proximity was all that was required.

Mr Cranshaw activated the Resonator Disruptor and made his way to the door. He unlocked the door with the key he had liberated from the Major-General's coat pocket, earlier in the day. Revolver in hand, he strode across the hall toward the parlour - where the object of his revenge would now be in a hypnotic thrall.

His skin tingled; twelve months of planning had finally reached its denouement. With proof of his invention's success, Cranshaw would receive a Fellowship in the Royal Society. They could not deny him now.

He opened the parlour door, and raised his pistol for the *coup de gras*, only to find all was not as it should be. The wife sat on the chaise; smiling. Staring. Unaware. Subject B.01 looked at him briefly and blinked. The Major-General slapped his paper on his knees and peered at him.

"Mr Cranshaw? What is the meaning of this intrusion?" he bellowed.

"No!" Mr Cranshaw squeezed the trigger and shot wildly, shattering a glass vase on the mantelpiece. "You're supposed to be—" His skin burned. "Why aren't you under the thrall of the Inducer? The experiments are a success. I have the notes to prove it."

With astonishing speed for a septuagenarian, the Major-General sprang from his chair and flanked Cranshaw, easily overpowering him, then knocked away the revolver, and manoeuvred the scientist into a headlock.

His wife remained motionless, her eyes now closed, apparently oblivious to the commotion.

Cranshaw struggled to free himself. The Major-General tightened his grip.

"The purring... Didn't you touch the cat?" asked Cranshaw.

"Don't be daft, man! Why would I do that?"

"People pay a fortune for a black. They're good luck," replied Cranshaw. He scratched the Major-General's arm.

The Major-General let out a raucous laugh and moved his head to scrutinise his attacker's face.

"There's no substitute for thorough research, Mister Cranshaw. If you had done it properly, you would know my forbears considered them bad luck, a sentiment reinforced by your current predicament, I would say." He glanced at his wife and frowned. "Elizabeth?"

There was no reply.

"What have you done to her?" He twisted Cranshaw's arms behind his back and held both wrists with one hand. With the other, he reached for his pipe and threw it at the cat. Startled, it hissed and jumped off his wife's lap. "Elizabeth!"

Elizabeth blinked, shook her head, and slowly turned to face him.

"Elizabeth, call the Constabulary," he hissed.

The Major-General hugged his wife as she sobbed quietly. The cat climbed onto the chaise, circled twice and settled on the warm spot she'd vacated. It blinked its amber eyes slowly at Mr Cranshaw as the Constable clamped the metal cuffs on his wrists and led him away.

The Major-General examined the small brass device confiscated from Mr Cranshaw, certain it could be put to use.

THE END

Right on Time

1890s, Adelaide

Steam hissed; scalding liquid spat from the joints. Saffie grabbed another damp rag and pressed it against the rattling pipe. Liquid seeped into her thick leather gloves. She winced as heat wrapped around her hand.

"Roland, we haven't got all day." She glared across the room at her brother, cowering behind a bench.

Roland swallowed and approached the contraption. He glanced over the array of buttons and levers on its panel, brushed his hand through his hair and grimaced. "Which one, Saffie?"

"The red one. Push the red one!"

Roland slammed the oversized red button, ducked to avoid another surge of pressurised vapour and backed away from the contraption.

The pressure eased under Saffie's palm. "Hand me the wrench."

Roland asked as he plopped the wrench into her outstretched hand. "Will it still work?"

A final wisp of steam escaped from the coupling as Saffie tightened the nut. She nodded.

"It should suffice."

A bell tinkled on the wall behind them.

"And just in time, it seems," she replied.

Saffie peeled off her gloves, tossed them onto the bench and examined the contraption.

Liquid whispered along the pipe into a large copper plated cistern sitting atop a large oak box. Gauge needles flickered as the pressure started to rise again. The contraption jiggled rhythmically. Saffie flicked the switch next to the red button. A steady stream of auburn liquid poured from a side spigot, filling a copper pot.

Saffie straightened her skirts and smiled. "Fetch the good china for our guests, Roland."

THE END

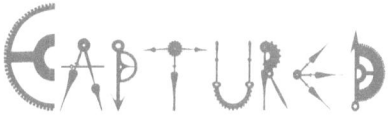

CAPTURED

1909, Adelaide

lsie picked her way along a steep, stony track past an old silver mine. Her foot rolled and slipped on the loose rocks, depositing her on a thicket of thorny Christmas Bush. She rubbed her ankle and groaned. When she'd joined the Department of Curiosities, she'd thought she'd travel the world, like her mother had, not be traipsing the Hills looking for a... well, she wasn't exactly sure what.

She consulted the scribbled map she'd discovered in her mother's diary hidden in the Department archives; it was the only clue to her mother's last days. She'd recognised her mother's hand-written notes, dated the day before her disappearance. And there was a name: Francis Whyte, a fellow operative accused of theft who'd absconded two years earlier.

Elsie read the notes again. Past the silver mine and half-way up the next hill there'd be a well. She shoved the map back into her shoulder satchel, grabbed a sturdy stick, and hauled herself to her feet. She was almost there.

The track continued into the scrub past the mine.

She stopped at a large clump of impenetrable bushland guarded by a stand of tea tree. An infestation of lantana and bougainvillea had dragged one of the gum trees down at a sharp angle, and buried its branches into the remains of a crushed fireplace.

Hidden beneath overgrown vines were the surprisingly intact stone walls of a small cottage. Elsie inserted her gloved hand into a thin patch of bougainvillea. A thorn pierced her glove and gouged her skin. She whipped off her glove and sucked the wound, then peeled back the vines and felt along the wall until she found a niche in the stone.

There was a faint click. The front door creaked open, as if inviting her in.

Elsie hesitated. If her mother had been here the day she disappeared, then she must be cautious. There was no telling what treachery awaited her. She dusted the pale stone dust from her hand and slipped over the threshold.

Another click as she stepped inside the main room. The door slammed shut behind her. The room was dim. Elsie waited for her vision to adjust.

A large fireplace dominated the room. In the firebox was a pile of leaves and twigs held back by a rusting fire screen. To her left was a door with a crust of disintegrating white paint.

Shrouded shapes covered with years of dust were recognisable: a small dining table and chairs in the middle of the room. Near the window was a partly-uncovered side table.

On the far side of the room, next to a second door, was a sash window. The lower window pane had been smashed long ago, breached by a gum branch. Shredded red linen hung from the window frame, casting crimson shadows across the scuffed floor boards. Torn books were scattered across the floor.

Elsie picked up one of the intact tomes - a first edition. She wiped off the cover and slipped it into her satchel.

Her ankle twinged as she crept past shroud-covered furniture towards the side table.

Glass crunched underfoot near the window. A broken light tube lay on the floor. Faded footprints disturbed shards.

Someone had already been here.

On the side table was a battered clockwork bird in a rusted cage, a small jeweller's screwdriver lay beside it. Oxidised springs and cogs littered the base of the cage. Elsie turned the small key at its base. The bird's wing twitched, then seized. A woeful song issued from the disembowelled body, and slowed to a drawn-out warble as it wound down.

The leaves in the fire grate rustled and exploded. The grate toppled and clattered onto the tiled floor. An enormous rat scurried across the floor boards, under the closest furniture cover, and darted between the exposed turned-wooden legs of one of the furniture-ghosts.

Elsie recoiled into a low-hanging cobweb and rammed her back into the doorknob behind her. She hissed as she scraped off the sticky strands. "It was a rat, you idiot."

There was an ominous-sounding clunk under her feet. The door latch thunked.

Flecks of rust peppered both the doorknob and the surrounding rosary. She turned the knob and pushed. Peeling paint crumbled under her palm.

The door didn't budge.

Pain pricked her bare fingers. She sucked a quick breath through her teeth as she pulled larger bits of rust from her skin, and wiped away beads of blood with a handkerchief.

Movement caught the corner of her eye. The rat scampered across the floor and under the side table to sanctuary. The cover cloth tugged in its wake. The cage on the side table shuddered. The mechanical bird squawked, and jettisoned another spring. Its unsteady twittering cut off with a metallic snap.

Tap, tap.

The noise was faint, from the other side of the room.

Tap. Tap, tap.

Another rat?

Elsie moved closer. There was nothing there except the second door. It had a rusted door knob and doorplate, similar to the first, but this one had a keyhole. She fetched a pocket-sized brass case from her satchel. She rolled her thumb over a dial on the side. The end slid open. An array of long thin picks cycled through one by one. Elsie selected a pair, slid them into the keyhole. The tumblers clicked into place. She grinned.

The lighting tube rolled.

Elsie jerked her hand away from the doorknob. She froze, expecting to hear another mechanical to activate. There was nothing. Not a sound; only the tap tap beckoning her to move forward.

Her muscles relaxed. She was getting paranoid. She reached for the knob. It turned easily; the door swung half-open.

Her hand throbbed. She rubbed her fingers. Was it wise to continue? Her training had taught her to pause, evaluate, then engage - only if necessary. But the map in her satchel indicated her mother intended to investigate the cottage, and her only clue about her mother's disappearance.

Another tap beckoned her closer. She *had* to go.

Cogs whirred in the wall. A faint tang of sulphur caught her nostrils. A grating sound rumbled under her feet. The door slammed behind her.

The room was dark. A sliver of light crept along a crack on the far wall. The tapping originated there. Shapes formed in the shadows: a chair in the centre of the room, a cabinet, a desk under the window.

A glint of light winked at her to the left.

Elsie slipped on a pair of night goggles from her satchel and moved closer to the sliver of light.

There was a faint, uneven whir. A low grind vibrated along the far wall. The window shutter jolted. Wood slats clattered. The left shutter slapped open; the right side stuck, wedged on a tree branch.

A blaze of sudden light flooded her vision. Glare flared across the goggle lenses. Metal screeched as hidden cogs ground to a halt. Elsie shielded her eyes, lunged towards the sound, and tore off the goggles.

Her leg knocked hard against the corner of a solid object, jarring her injured ankle. A ripple of pain shot up her calf.

A shaft of light illuminated the left side of the room, partly blocked by overgrown gum and tea trees. A tendril of lantana snaked its way through the smashed window.

Scratches scored the remaining glass.

A warm gully breeze whistled through the room. The branch tapped the desk. Papers rustled. Light reflected off the glass curiosity cabinet next to the chair, in time with the moving branches.

She leaned against the desk to relieve the pressure on her foot. An expensive-looking glass paperweight with a flower inside it held down a scattered pile of papers. A used metal nib and holder was overturned. Ink had seeped into the green leather writing surface and the clung to the glass - dried long ago. Two silver boxes sat to the right; one filled with pencil stubs, the other with fresh pen nibs. On the left was an overturned photograph in a small, silver case.

Elsie picked up the photograph; a greyed image of a blonde woman and a man in a dark, three-piece suit, the lacquer peeling in the corners.

The woman was seated. Her braided hair was pulled high, with long ringlets falling over a high-collared bodice trimmed with velvet and pleated edging. White lace peeked out from under her cuffs. A chatelaine hung at her belt. She held the hand of the man standing next to her - her husband, judging by his age. His long, wiry beard was neatly trimmed, his long fringe flipped back from his face. He looked familiar.

She pulled her mother's diary from her satchel. A cabinet card was stuffed in the pages. Her pulse raced. It was the same man; the missing operative her mother had been investigating.

Elsie tucked the cabinet card into her satchel, and shuffled through the papers on the desk, searching for information - anything that would explain why her mother had come here. But there was nothing. She pulled the handle of the left desk drawer. It was stuck fast. She tried the other one. Same. She slipped the blade of her boot knife along the edge of the drawer. It slipped smoothly along the crevice. She tugged it again. Locked? But there was no keyhole. She ran her hand along the smooth mahogany, to check for secret compartments. Again, nothing.

She huffed, and surveyed the illuminated half of the room. The single, central chair was upholstered in padded red velvet. Next to it was a curiosity cabinet, full of mementos and knickknacks. A painted, canvas backdrop lined the side wall next to the now-closed door. A bookshelf overflowing with leather-bound volumes hugged the wall.

A mysterious object as tall as a man, cloaked in a long black cloth lurked in the shadows on the opposite side of the room.

Elsie tested her weight on her ankle, limped towards it. The smell of sulphur was stronger here. She yanked the black cloth. She spluttered, dropped the cloth, and fanned away the particles of flash-powder and dust.

Atop a wooden tripod was an old-style camera made of polished mahogany, with several lenses encased in etched brass tubes: two small ancillary lenses above an over-sized main lens. A large glass plate was slotted into its cradle. Frayed wires trailed along a metal arm attached to the tripod to the camera shutter and connected to the electrodes of an old corroding battery.

Elsie frowned. Why would her mother visit a photographer?

Perhaps the bookshelf's contents would provide some information? The last dozen volumes - all bound in black - had no titles on the spine. Elsie removed the first one from its slipcase.

On the first page was a purplish-brown photograph, its highlights tinged yellow with age. A seated man stared into the camera, looking very uncomfortable; his hands were clenched, his eyes wide. A hint of reflected flash peeked out from under his lapel. Hand-written beneath it: *#1 A.S. 17th February, 1898*. The next photograph was a man, also seated, inscribed: *#2 T.W. 1st March, 1898*. Both dated two years before her mother disappeared.

She pulled out the next album and flipped through more photographs, each dated 1899.

Pain gripped her ankle. She pulled out the third untitled album and collapsed into the chair and loosened her boot lace. She re-examined all three albums. The first had page after page of portraits, each in chronological order, the last dated 17th December, 1898. The second album's photographs were also in chronological order, all dated 1899, numbered, and labelled with initials.

Elsie opened the third black-bound volume. The date on the first page was 4th January, 1900. Nine years ago; the year mother disappeared. She flicked through the photos... February... March. Then no more photos. The next two pages held only notations: *#18 E.W. 14th March* - the day before her mother disappeared - and *#19 M.M. 15th March* - the day her mother disappeared.

She flipped back through the pages. In every photograph, the subject was seated on a chair; the very same chair on which she now sat. And in all but the first, the curiosity cabinet was beside them.

Elsie extracted a magnifying lorgnette from under her linen coat and examined the images closely. With each photo, there appeared to be more items in the cabinet.

She wiped off the fine layer of dust on the glass of the curiosity cabinet and peered inside. An early version of self-inking pen, hatpins, various brooches, a moustache comb, a chatelaine, and–

She leaned closer.

...a Department of Curiosities badge. No operative would part with their badge willingly.

Elsie lifted the catch, removed the badge from the cabinet, and turned it over. A thread of navy-blue linen was caught in the clasp. She examined it with her lorgnette for the three micro-engraved numbers that would identify the operative who wore it. *Three, one, three.* She would look it up on her return. She clipped it under her jacket lapel, next to her own, and snapped the photo album closed. Dust blew up her nose. She stifled a cough.

Glass clinked in the deep shadows on the other side of the room.

Elsie was on her feet. Her ankle buckled. She cursed and grabbed the back of the chair.

A rolling sound followed, then silence, and the crash of shattering glass.

There was a faint squeak, the scratch of tiny claws on the floorboards.

Elsie groaned. The rat had followed her.

A sharp chemical stench enveloped her. It burned the back of her throat. She gagged, grabbed her handkerchief, and slapped it over her nose and mouth. Her eyes watered as she stumbled into the darkness, searching with her free hand.

The sound of dripping drew her to the site of the accident.

The air was more pungent here. She searched the darkness. Metal rattled. Her fingers sloshed in liquid. She flicked off the liquid, and clasped the handkerchief tighter over her nostrils.

She felt her way along the cold, metallic surface until she found a small box. A smooth cylindrical tube was attached to the top. A small switch was embedded next to it. She flipped it.

There was a click and a loud hiss. A flicker of harsh, pale blue light crackled along a glass cylinder, filling the shadows. It flickered for a few seconds, then settled into a continuous hum, revealing rows of bottles - some toppled over - along an aluminium bench spanning the entire wall. White fluid oozed over the bench and trickled off the edge. Several large rectangular trays filled with liquid were set up in front of the bottles. Fresh splashes of dark liquid had splattered over the bench near the last tray.

Elsie rubbed grit from her fingertips where it had stained them pale grey. She sniffed it. Odourless.

On the left of the bench was a tall container with a tap positioned above the first tray. To its left was a large, rectangular wooden box with brass fixtures. A glass photographic plate sat on top of it. To the right of the trays was a washing contraption with a metal box attached to the wall. A tap sat above a deep tray, with a pivoting open-topped box. A lever on the side was attached to a rusted, circular timer. Beyond that was a smudged cloth, and a curled photograph pegged to a wire rack suspended from the wall.

As Elsie reached for the photograph, there was a jarring screech of twigs scraping on glass. She cringed. The last tray shuddered. The liquid inside trembled. A corner of paper broke the surface.

She extracted the slippery paper from the dish and shook off the excess liquid. The greyed image was in poor condition. She peered at the print under the light tube. She could just work out the shadowy outline of a figure.

She turned the tap of the washing contraption. Pipes knocked. Water gurgled from the faucet, filled the agitator box, and overflowed. She slipped the paper in, and cranked the lever on the side. Gears whined. The timer clicked. Water shivered in the box as it began to rock back and forth.

The timer continued. *Tick, click. Tick, click.*

Elsie turned her attention to the curled photograph on the rack. It was the woman in the tintype portrait from the desk. But in the desk portrait, she seemed happy, confident; in this one she was about thirty years older. Her face was pale, her cheeks sunken, and there were dark circles under her eyes. A hint of trepidation clouded them. She clenched her hands in her lap. And there was something missing: her chatelaine.

Elsie examined the tintype from her satchel. The chatelaine in the photograph was the same as in the curiosity cabinet.

Gears grated. The washing contraption halted. Elsie snatched up the photograph before it washed into the lower tray and escaped through the waste pipe, and pressed it dry with the cloth from the rack.

It was a photograph of a woman jumping towards the camera. The chair was blurred, falling over. The shape of her face seemed familiar. Elsie's heart raced.

The inscription in the photograph album... *M.M.*? Surely that wasn't—?

She couldn't be sure. The image was too degraded; she needed to see the original negative. She snatched up the photographic plate from the box at the opposite end of the bench. Etched onto the glass was a date: *15th March, 1900*.

Elsie examined it with her lorgnette. The facial features were blurred, but it was—

She gasped. "Mother!"

Her mother *had* been here the day she disappeared.

Elsie ran her eye over the image again. Her mother's Department of Curiosities badge was gone, and there was a tear on her jacket, matching the thread on the clasp; the badge from the cabinet must belong to her mother.

Elsie swallowed, and glanced at the trophies in the cabinet. Had she stumbled over one of The Society's kidnap plots? A multiple murderer? Either could explain the mysterious disappearances over the past few years. The Department had sent several operatives to investigate. If the photos were a record of those missing, the Department had to be informed.

The image on the plate flickered. Elsie jumped, catching the glass plate before it hit the ground.

She sighed in relief, hobbled across the room, and crumpled into the armchair.

Another flicker of movement flashed across the glass plate. The image cleared.

Elsie cleared her throat. Perhaps the chemical fumes were stronger than she'd thought? She blew away the layer of dust covering the image, and peered closer. Her mother's hands gesticulated wildly in her direction.

Elsie's blood ran cold. Her mother's mouth was moving, forming words: help.

"That's imposs—"

The rat skittered behind her. Its claws tugged her stockings as it ran over her foot, sending a crawling shiver up her calf. She flinched, and kicked it away, catapulting into the air towards the camera. It landed hard against one of the tripod legs and ricocheted under the bench.

The tripod scraped across the floorboards.

"No!" Elsie lunged towards it, grabbed for the discarded cover cloth as she slid forward.

The camera listed forward.

She sucked in a sharp breath and jerked her hand away from the camera.

The rat screeched.

The camera crashed to the floor. Glass shattered. There was a blinding flash of light.

The stench of sulphur filled the air. Elsie panicked. She searched blindly for the photographic plate. Shards of glass sliced her fingers.

A clammy wave of nausea flooded over her. She scrambled to her feet as the lights faded from her vision.

The glass was remnants from the damaged camera lenses. The photographic plate was upended on the armchair. And the rat was gone.

THE END

AFTERWORD

(Why I write the things I write…)

Cogs and Conspiracies is a collection a long time in the making. Ever since I had the idea for the first story in my years alternate historical steampunk world, *The Department of Curiosities* (left unfinished for five years), I had a grand plan: a vision of writing steampunk stories set in Australia. At the time, there wasn't weren't many Aussie steampunk stories, and my confidence was almost non-existent.

Back then, authors were discouraged, by traditional publishing houses, from writing stories set in Australia as they 'didn't sell.' Determined to forge ahead with my plan, I started to write *The Department of Curiosities*. The story is initially set in London (a common setting for steampunk stories) and finished with a dirigible trip to Australia.

For various reasons (listed below) I couldn't finish the steampunk then. My head was in a dark place and definitely not conducive to a whimsical adventure.

I turned to a short story I'd written in 2013. *An Eye for Detail* had been shortlisted in the *Australian Literature*

Review's murder mystery short story competition that year. It was about a nineteenth century widow, forbidden from pursuing her chosen career, forced into a more acceptable career as an optician (permitted as she was a widow). Very quickly she's embroiled in a murder mystery involving local homeless children.

The main character's name was Viola Stewart.

The story became part of my first book *Doctor Jack & Other Tales*, published in 2015.

Warning:
if you haven't read Doctor Jack & Other Tales. SPOILERS FOLLOW:

In the end, Viola faces the murderer and loses an eye in the process.

So much of this story stemmed from my crushing feeling of hopelessness and lack of power to control my own life. No doubt, I excised her eye in direct response to my own situation at the time.

And it felt good.

I found delving into my characters' psyche strangely cathartic. As I did so, I examined my own mental health, my past, my future. The series became slowly 'lighter' in tone with each book.

The main stories in *The Adventures of Viola Stewart* are set over the period of 1888 (Jack the Ripper), 1889, and 1890. 1890 brought with it the Great World Fair (*Exposition Universelle*) in Paris. I allowed the story to embrace the time of wonder and invention, but still there were undercurrents of betrayal and conspiracy. *The Illusioneer & Other Tales* –

the third and final book in the series – was first published in 2017.

All three books were re-released with new covers in 2022.

2018: I returned to *The Department of Curiosities*, but still, I couldn't face Tillie Meriwether's bravery and zeal to find answers. Instead, I borrowed strength from the women in my family. *Aunt Enid: Protector Extraordinaire* was inspired by my own Great Aunt Enid and my grandmother, and set in my adopted home of Adelaide. I intended Aunt Enid to be a cosy mystery with a fantasy twist, but the humour was darker than even I expected, definitely not the light-hearted fare of American cosies – but more in keeping with the emerging darker Australian cosy mysteries genre.

During 2013 and 2019 I wrote several short stories, many set in my book worlds. Both my cosy mystery world and my steampunk world grew with each new characters explored. These stories enabled me to finish *The Department of Curiosities.* I finally felt emotionally ready to do Tillie's story justice. I revisited the first draft and I rewrote over half of it (there are still two notebooks missing).

After seven years, I'd finally achieved what I'd started back in 2012: a steampunk story in Australia.

After *The Department of Curiosities* was published, I had fun exploring my steampunk world and discovering more characters. Three of these short stories have found their way to this collection: *All that Glitters*, *Right on Time*, and T*he Feline Principle. Incoming* was originally written as a 2021 Patreon short story reward, and finally *Captured* was added this year.

This collection contains stories of a mine in the Adelaide Hills, the perils of clothes washing, some friendly cats, solving a cold case puzzle, and of course – making the perfect cup of tea…

All but one of these are set in Australia.

All that Glitters is set in the tail end of the Gold Rush era of South Australia. It was first published in *Den of Antiquity* in 2016. (ISBN: 978-0995276727), an anthology produced by Scribblers Den, a group of fellow steampunk authors who encouraged me in my writing journey. I wanted to add an Aussie flavour, so I wrote the story inspired by both the women whose husband's left them behind when they left to follow the gold rush to Victoria, and research I'd done on the Lady Alice Mine, a gold and copper mine in the mid-1800s in Humbug Scrub in the Adelaide Hills. Those of you who've read my Aunt Enid Mysteries may recognise Humbug Scrub as it's featured in A Fey Tale.

Incoming is set about 20 years later, again in the Adelaide Hills. It was also inspired by the women left behind during the gold rush in Victoria.

The Feline Principle is set in 1870s London. (In the 1st eBook edition of Cogs and Conspiracies, it was mis-dated at 1890, and out of order.) The story was inspired by an online comment, someone was freaking out about black cats. Personally, I love black cats. I did a little research and confirmed they are not bad luck in all cultures. So, of course, I had to add a steampunk twist…

Right on Time was first published in *Denizens of Steam*, the Scribblers Den anthology of 2015. (ISBN: 9781311741042) It's a bit of fun and, let's face it, I love a good cup of tea.

Captured was written specifically for the collection. It was inspired by a Furious Fiction (by Australian Writers Centre) prompt. The story grew. I wove in some easter eggs from both *The Department of Curiosities,* and *Doctor Jack & Other Tales*. entrenching it in the former's extended timeline.

I love stories with easter eggs – and I love writing them.

All That Glitters © 2016 Karen J Carlisle
Incoming © 2021 Karen J Carlisle
The Feline Principle © 2013/2020 Karen J Carlisle
Right on Time © 2015 Karen J Carlisle
Captured © 2023 Karen J Carlisle

My writing journey;
a bit about mental health.

I often talk about mental health (someone has to). Not only does it highlight challenges many of us face, but it helps me process my feelings and thought processes.

I studied for my BAppSc at Queensland Institute of Technology and started work as an optometrist in 1986. (My hand shakes less when I say that now…)

Back in 2012 my professional world seemed to be crumbling. Anxiety and PTSD triggered by my then-work environment had almost crippled me (both mentally and physically). I was put on Work Cover in late 2012. This was the beginning of years (and continuing) appointments with specialists, for anxiety (PTSD was finally diagnosed five years later), referrals to a pain physiologist, psychologists, and neurologist.

After a six-month break, I transitioned back to work part-time. And struggled.

I was advised to "follow your bliss." (Not, 'what made me happy', but 'what made me content.')

But what the heck was my bliss? Books. Writing.

I dusted off thirty-year-old notes for a fantasy novel I'd always wanted to write. It was high fantasy, with a touch of humour…

Humour; I wasn't really feeling that at the time.

Then I saw a photograph: a mechanical eye. I started jotting down notes for another story. Nothing like I'd written before. Turns out it was steampunk. That was the beginnings of *The Department of Curiosities*. I wrote a first draft in my lunch breaks – the highlight of my days. I lived for that moment. I scrawled my way through various school notebooks purloined from our offspring, and managed to get within four chapters of the end of that first draft.

But my situation hadn't improved. I fought the 'flight' response every time I arrived at work.

My mental health spiralled. Migraines came with increasing frequency. There were nightmares, and post-midnight ambulance trips to various hospital with anxiety attacks mimicking heart attacks. Thankfully (?), most of the symptoms were anxiety-related.

Just eighteen months later, I was a wreck. I was in a dark place. There was no silver lining, no room for 'bliss'.

I stopped writing.

There were more trips to hospital with scary anxiety attacks, culminating in referral to a heart specialist with cardiograms and stress tests.

In 2014, in excruciating back pain, I quit my career. A total break. Almost anything eye-related triggered me. But, what could I do now? I was on the wrong side of forty. I'd been in the same job for twenty-eight years. I was broken. To this day, the nightmares persist.

'*What have you always wanted to do?*' I was asked.

Too many things. I joked about my dream jobs: writer, artist, cinematographer, astronaut/astro-physicist, and being *Doctor Who*'s next companion…

I eventually turned to my greatest love (other than my Dearheart and offspring): books. In this case, it was writing, which I discovered was extremely therapeutic.

Fortunately, my family was (and still are) extremely supportive. They had no qualms about me quitting a well-paid career for a writer's life. (Though I do wonder if – no, I know – my Dearheart has plans to accompany me to the Green Room if I should ever become 'famous'. He has many favourite authors he'd like to meet.)

Slowly, I could see the light at the end of the tunnel. Writing helps me. Through it I explore the darkness, the 'long dark tea-time of the soul' as Douglas Adams puts it. I delve into not just what and how characters think, but why they think it (myself included). Only recently, I've experienced fleeting, long-forgotten moments of joy. I couldn't have gotten there without my Dearheart and my writing.

To say steampunk saved my life is possibly an exaggeration. But writing steampunk has been cathartic, and helped me rediscover a little whimsical joy in life.

I hope these stories give you a little joy as well.

ACKNOWLEDGEMENTS

Thank you to David Carlisle, Sharon Kemmett and the steampunk community for their support. Some of these short stories were originally available as Patreon rewards.

The following shorts were previously published in anthologies:

Right on Time was first published in *Denizens of Steam,* Scribblers Den anthology, 2015. ISBN: 9781311741042)

All That Glitters was first published in *Den of Antiquity,* Scribblers Den anthology, 2016. ISBN: 978-0995276727)

This print edition is based on the second edition eBook, with the corrected timeline, and order, of the stories.

About the Author

Karen J Carlisle lives in Adelaide with her family and the ghost of her ancient Devon Rex cat. She loves fantasy fiction, gardening, historical re-creation, and steampunk and can often be found plotting fantastical, piratic or airship adventures. Karen has always loved chocolate and rarely refuses a cup of tea. She is not keen on South Australian summers.

www.karenjcarlisle.com

You can support Karen at:
https://www.patreon.com/KarenJCarlisle
https://ko-fi.com/karenjcarlisle

Follow Karen at:
www.goodreads.com/KarenJCarlisle
https://www.instagram.com/karenjcarlisle/
https://www.tiktok.com/@karenjcarlisle
https://www.facebook.com/KarenJCarlisle
https://twitter.com/kjcarlisle

Sign up for Karen's newsletter:
https://karenjcarlisle.com/sign-up-email-list/

Other works by Karen J Carlisle

Available in paperback and eBook:
The Adventures of Viola Stewart series:
Doctor Jack & Other Tales: Journal #1
Eye of the Beholder & Other Tales: Journal #2
The Illusioneer & Other Tales: Journal #3

The Aunt Enid Mysteries
Aunt Enid: Protector Extraordinaire
A Fey Tale

The Department of Curiosities
The Department of Curiosities

Available as eBooks:
Short Story Collections
With a Twist of the Nib: For when time is short
Another Twist of the Nib: Shorter Tales with a Darker Twist
Quarantine Reads: Escape to Adventure
Cogs and Conspiracies: A collection of steampunk short stories

Mrs Hudson Investigates
Mrs Hudson Investigates
The Case of the Forgotten Letter

Coming soon
Blood Ties: A mini adventure #1
Against the Empire

www.ingramcontent.com/pod-product-compliance
Lightning Source LLC
Chambersburg PA
CBHW020535120726
47904CB00003B/1081